Our New Love

—A Short Story—

The Bradens

Love in Bloom Series

Melissa Foster

ISBN-13: 978-1-941480-45-8
ISBN-10: 1941480454

OUR NEW LOVE

Cover Design: Elizabeth Mackey Designs

WORLD LITERARY PRESS
PRINTED IN THE UNITED STATES OF AMERICA

Dear Readers,

Thank you so much for your encouragement and ongoing support for the Love in Bloom series. I love hearing from you, and I hope you enjoy catching up with your favorite characters.

If this is your first introduction to the Bradens and Remingtons, please note that this is a **short story**, not a full-length novel. *Our New Love* follows Savannah (Braden) and Jack Remington, the couple featured in *Bursting With Love* (The Bradens, a full-length novel). The Bradens and Remingtons are part of the Love in Bloom big family romance collection featuring several families (Snow Sisters, The Bradens, The Remingtons, Seaside Summers, The Ryders, Harborside Nights, Wild Boys, and Bad Boys). Characters from each family series appear in future Love in Bloom books. Love in Bloom books can be enjoyed as stand-alone novels or as part of the series.

See Melissa's website to start the Love in Bloom series FREE. www.melissafoster.com/LIBFree

Sign up for my newsletter to be notified of new releases and events:
www.melissafoster.com/newsletter

Happy reading!
Melissa

Chapter One

WEDDINGS ALWAYS DID Savannah Remington in, and the double wedding of her brothers-in-law Rush and Dex to their fiancées, Jayla Stone and Ellie Parker, completely drained her. Maybe her pregnancy hormones were making her even more emotional than usual. At eight and a half months pregnant, she felt like a big-bellied puddle of tears. At least the wedding had gone off without a hitch, despite the chilly October afternoon. Her brother Treat Braden, the owner of the Colorado resort where the celebration was taking place, had certainly outdone himself this time. The elegant white tent he'd had erected on the property overlooked the Colorado Mountains, where Savannah and her husband, Jack, were planning to spend the week at their secluded little cabin in the woods. They were leaving right after the wedding, although from the looks of it, the wedding might never officially end. Rush and Jayla were glued together on the dance floor beside Dex and Ellie, looking stunning in their tuxes and wedding gowns. They were surrounded by the rest of the Remington clan and their significant others, as well as too many Bradens to count. The families—extended and immediate—had grown as close as families could be over the last few years, and Savannah could not have been happier.

"Angel." Jack's arms slipped around her from behind, embracing their unborn child as he embraced his wife.

Savannah turned in his arms. His midnight-blue eyes held even more love than they had when they'd met, when they'd married, and even more than when they'd found out they were going to have a baby. He never failed to surprise her with an endless well of emotions, especially after he'd overcome so much. Jack had lost his first wife in a car accident two years before he'd met Savannah, and it was Savannah's love that had helped heal him.

"Dance with me?" he asked, before pressing his lips to hers.

He always knew what she needed. As much as she'd helped him heal, from the first time they'd met, he'd been her rock. In good times and bad, he was so in tune to her needs and always willing to give more of himself, regardless of whether she was happy, sad, angry, or bored.

Savannah wiped her happy tears and sniffed back the emotions threatening to steal her voice. She nodded and took his outstretched hand.

"I'm sorry. I don't mean to be so emotional," she said as she wound her arms around his neck and ran her fingers through his thick dark hair. Jack was six four and built like a lumberjack, thickly muscled, solid, and stable. He'd earned that incredible physique when he was in the Special Forces, and as a survival guide his ruggedness was tested and revitalized on a weekly basis. Of course, with their baby due soon, Jack hadn't left Savannah's side in more than a week, and he'd already cleared his schedule for several more weeks so he could be with her even after the birth. Most women's mothers would offer to help with a new baby, but Savannah had lost her mother to cancer when she was too young to remember her. With five brothers, Savannah had plenty of sisters-in-law who had offered to come stay with them when the baby was born, not to mention her best friend and coworker at her law firm, Aida Strong. But Jack insisted he wanted to be there every step of the way. She loved him even more for that.

Jack pressed another soft kiss to her lips. "Don't be. Weddings always get to that giant heart of yours. It makes you even more beautiful."

Savannah rested her head on his chest. These last two weeks with Jack had brought them even closer together, regardless of how emotional she'd been. She wondered if her emotions would level off after the baby was born. *Another two weeks.* She smiled with the thought, although her doctor had told her that it could be even longer with a first baby. She was just overjoyed about finally meeting the little person she and Jack had created.

Savannah spotted her aunt Catherine and Jack's mother, Joanie, across the room, chatting with a handful of her cousins. The two women were shaking their heads but smiling, a look she'd seen often from the women who had raised such big clans.

Treat leaned in close to Jack. "How's she holding up?" He was dancing with his wife, Max, and holding their youngest, Dylan, in one arm, as he asked Jack the question. His ever-watchful eyes skirted over Jack's shoulder to his daughter, Adriana, named for their mother, who was smiling and chatting away while dancing with their father, Hal.

"I'm fine," Savannah said, feeling more like herself again. After their mother had died, Treat had looked after Savannah and their other four siblings with eagle eyes, too. Now the dark eyes that all the Braden men shared came back to her with an assessing gaze.

"Vanny, are you sure you're feeling okay other than the tears?" Treat asked, before pressing a kiss to Dylan's chubby cheek.

"Yeah, actually, I feel great. You know how weddings affect me."

"Then can I steal you for a minute?" Max asked. Max was a petite little thing. Savannah had several inches on her, and as Max pulled her from Jack's grasp, he held her fingertips until Max tugged her away with a smile. "I'll bring her back. I promise."

They disappeared into the crowd and joined the other girls on the opposite side of the tent. Their families had really grown. A small family wedding meant Jack's five siblings and their significant others, and not only Savannah's immediate family, but their eighteen Braden cousins. And that was just on the Braden side. The Remingtons had invited their cousins from the East Coast, as well. It had been a tough decision for Rush and Jayla to exclude their friends from the Olympic ski team, and for Dex and Ellie to exclude their closest friends, all of whom had hoped to honor them. But they wanted the joint wedding to be small, and even with just family, there were close to a hundred people there.

"Savannah!" Siena, Savannah's sister-in-law, was a gorgeous model who'd recently wed her fiancée, Cash Ryder. She pulled Savannah from Max and wrapped her in her arms. "It's time to have some fun."

Savannah noticed the glint of mischief in the other girls' eyes. Her very pregnant sisters-in-law Jade and Lacy were huddled close to Riley, whispering and watching their handsome husbands, Savannah's older brothers Rex and Dane, who were busy chatting with Savannah's youngest brother, Hugh,

Jack's brother Sage, and his father, James. Riley's eyes were locked on Josh, who was standing just a few feet away, watching her right back as he chatted with Jack's brother Kurt and Kurt's wife, Leanna. The love in the room was overwhelming.

Savannah glanced back at the dance floor, where Brianna held her toddler, Christian, while dancing with her daughter, Layla, and Kate, Sage's fiancée. Jayla's sisters Mia and Jennifer were chatting with Savannah's cousins, but it was Jack who held her attention. He stood with his arms crossed and a serious look in his eyes as he talked with Savannah's cousins Nate, Cole, and Ty. Four gorgeous men, and the best-looking of them all was all hers.

"Stop staring at your hunka hunka burning love and pay attention." Siena turned her toward the girls, who were quickly flocking around them, along with Joanie and Catherine. "So, here's the plan. Now that the cake has been cut and the afternoon is winding down, all of us girls are going to the spa. Well, not Ellie and Jayla, of course. They're going to christen their wedding day." Siena smiled at the brides, who both turned a pretty shade of pink.

"Thanks for that, Siena," Jayla teased. "Because everyone needs to know *exactly* what we're doing tonight."

Joanie laid a gentle hand on Jayla's shoulder. "Sweetheart, it's your wedding day. Enjoy it." She turned a sarcastic tone to Siena. "But you probably didn't need to announce it, honey."

"Oh, Mom." Siena waved her off and turned back to Savannah. "So? Spa in an hour?"

"I would love to, but I can't. Remember? Jack and I are going up to the cabin for the week. One last hurrah before the baby comes."

"I cannot wait to meet that baby." Catherine came to her

side and patted her belly. "I loved being pregnant so much."

"So do we," Lacy and Jade said in unison.

"But I need the spa today." Lacy pushed at her blond spiral curls, which had gotten even thicker with her pregnancy. "My feet are killing me."

"I would rather have Rexy massage my feet than someone I don't know," Jade said.

Savannah rolled her eyes, knowing the truth behind her statement—even though Jade probably *would* rather have Rex massage her than anyone else. "That's because my brother is too jealous to let any other man touch you."

"I happen to like Rexy's possessive side." Jade lifted her chin and wiggled her shoulders, as if she were saying, *So there!* Jade was the perfect match for her überalpha brother. They both laughed because it was true. Jack had a possessive side, too, and Savannah loved it as much as Jade loved Rex's.

"I can't believe your doctor allowed all this flying so late in your pregnancy," Max said.

"He seemed okay with it. He said the baby will probably be late anyway, since it's my first. Besides, Jack can fly us back lickety-split if I need him to." Jack was an excellent pilot, and Savannah trusted him one hundred percent. He'd never let anything happen to her or their unborn child.

"Speaking of Jack." Joanie's eyes lifted over Savannah's shoulder. "I couldn't be happier to see my son so in love, and *that's* a man in love if I ever saw one."

Savannah turned to see Jack heading in her direction, a white rose from one of the bouquets in his hand, a crooked grin on his handsome face. She hoped she was the only one who recognized the dark seduction in his eyes. Even pregnant, they couldn't get enough of each other. They made love nearly every day, and Jack spoiled her rotten afterward with warm showers, where he took his time, washing and loving her in equal measure, and they slept so close together that she thought he'd climb inside her with the baby if he could. There was no doubt she was one hell of a lucky woman.

Jack's eyes narrowed at his younger sister as he slipped one arm around Savannah's waist and held on tight. He pressed his lips to her cheek in a sweet kiss. "Are these ladies trying to steal you away from me?"

"They're going to the spa." Savannah turned toward him and touched his cheek. Even though he'd shaved for the wedding, sexy whiskers were already peppering his chiseled cheeks.

"If you want to go, angel, we can leave tomorrow for the cabin," he offered.

There was a rise of encouragement from the girls, but Savannah was tired. She'd been on her feet all day, and nothing sounded better than lying in Jack's arms before a roaring fire in their cabin, with no worries and no one to entertain or listen to but each other.

"Thanks, but I've been really looking forward to this."

"Party pooper," Siena teased as her burly firefighter husband, Cash, wrapped his strong arms around her from behind.

"Who's pooping on my girl's party?" Cash lifted his eyes to the girls.

"Savannah and Jack are leaving," Siena answered with a frown.

"I thought the guys were going out tonight?" Cash rose to his full height and tugged Siena in closer, whispering, "Does this mean we can head upstairs?"

Savannah knew that whisper was meant just for Siena to

hear, and when Jack squeezed her side, she realized he'd heard it, too. She touched Jack's cheeks again to get his attention.

"I'm ready to call it a day and head up to the cabin. Are you?"

A smile spread his full lips. "More than ready."

Chapter Two

IT HAD TAKEN Jack and Savannah almost an hour to say goodbye to everyone at the wedding and then another two hours to gather their things and get to the airport where Jack kept his bush plane. Jack had had his mechanic check out the plane the day before to ensure they wouldn't run into any issues, and as he helped Savannah with her seat belt, he ran his hands over her belly, then lowered his lips and pressed a kiss to it.

She brushed his hair off his forehead, and he stayed right there for a moment, reveling in her touch as he always did. He'd met Savannah at a time when he was as low as low could get, and her touch, her smile, her positive energy and deep understanding of all he'd been through had helped him heal. She'd shown him how to love again, and in doing so, had brought him back into the arms of his family and back into the world of the living. She'd truly been his angel.

"You are even more beautiful now than you were an hour ago."

"*Pfft.* You're such a flirt."

"Are you certain you want to do this? I know the doctor isn't worried, but are you? You're sure you don't want to be pampered at the spa instead?"

She shook her head and met him halfway for a kiss. "There's no place on earth I'd rather be than in our love nest in the woods. Besides, we first met on the mountain, so it's only fitting to spend a week up there before the baby comes. We'll have plenty of time for everything else when we return to New York and after the baby's born."

Twenty minutes later they were on their way.

"It's a little later than I would have liked to leave, but we should make it to the cabin before dark." Jack noted the grayish clouds moving in from the west as the sun began to dip from the sky. Savannah gazed out the window, and his chest swelled with love for her. He reached for her hand and gave it a quick squeeze.

"I remember when you flew the group up here the first time we met. I was so scared to fly in this little plane, and now I never think twice about it." She flashed a trusting smile. "Can you believe in a few weeks we'll meet our baby? We really should decide on names."

They'd been going around and around with names for months but had yet to settle on any.

"Well, we didn't want to know if we were having a boy or a girl, so would it be so bad not to decide on a name until he or she is born?" he suggested with a tease in his voice, because they'd been over this too many times to count. Savannah *liked* talking about names, even if they didn't know the sex of the baby. "I told you my take on names. If it's a boy, we should name him after your dad, to honor him, and if it's a girl, we can name her Haley or Halison or Hallelujah."

Savannah rolled her eyes. "Why are you so hung up on using my dad's name? Why not your father's name?"

"Because, Savannah, your father raised the woman I love, and although I love my folks, without Hal, there'd be no you. No us." He glanced at his beautiful wife. "I hope our baby feels as loved as you always have. I hope I can do our baby justice, and I hope he or she has your auburn hair and green eyes."

She rested her head back and closed her eyes as the plane bounced with turbulence.

"It's okay. I've got this," Jack assured her, bringing his attention back to the controls.

She rested her hands on her belly. "I know you do. To be honest, I hope our baby looks like you, and you're going to be an incredible father. You're the most loving man I know." Before he could say anything, she added, "I know my dad is a great father. He's gone through a lot, and he always put his family first, but so did yours. And, Jack, so do you. There's not a man on earth who could make me feel safer or more loved than you."

Jack soaked up her words as he kept them on a steady course and the ridge of their land came into view. He worried about being a good husband and a good father, but he knew that worry stemmed mostly from the loss of his first wife. When the tragic car accident had claimed his wife during a raging storm, just feet from their driveway, it had made Jack acutely aware of how powerless he was in the grand scheme of things. He rubbed the scar on his arm, where a thick piece of metal had cut him nearly to the bone as he'd dragged his wife's limp body from the burning car.

He had finally learned how to put the devastating images and emotions into a safer place, and now he forced them from his mind so he could focus on getting Savannah safely up the mountain. He'd feel better when she was in the cabin, toasty warm. He maneuvered the plane toward the landing strip as snow began to fall.

"It wasn't supposed to snow tonight, was it?" Savannah didn't sound worried, but Jack's gut was tightening.

"No, but that's Colorado for you. You sure you don't want to turn back? Just in case?"

"No. The baby's not due for two weeks, and I intend to chill out with my hubby for a week *here*. Then we can go home for the final countdown. Even if it snows, it won't be much. We would have heard about a storm front coming in." She pointed out the window. "Look, it's stopping. I think the weather fairies just got confused."

Jack lined the plane up with the landing strip, just over the hill from their cabin, feeling a little more at ease. She was right. They would have heard about a storm moving in. "Hang on, baby. We're going in."

Savannah closed her eyes and leaned back, her hands splayed protectively over her stomach. She'd never let on that landings still scared her. It was just one of the many things he adored about her. Savannah was the strongest woman he knew, and he'd known that from the moment he'd opened up to her about his wife's accident. Most women would want to bury a tragic past, feeling threatened or second best, but Savannah encouraged Jack to remember. She'd told him that he was the man he was because of what he'd gone through and that his life with Linda had helped turn him into the man he was. She wasn't threatened by his love for Linda, which would probably always be with him. She accepted his past as if she had loved Linda, too. Savannah was confident in their relationship, and had been since the beginning. She hadn't let Jack back off when he was being eaten alive by fear and self-loathing. Thank fucking God.

As the plane touched down, Savannah exhaled a loud breath, and her lips curved up in a smile. He settled the plane to a stop, and after cutting the engine and checking all his gear, he stepped from the plane and touched his fingers to the earth. He'd spent two years hiding from the world after the accident, and it was here he'd found his footing. He considered the mountain theirs, even though they owned only two hundred acres. It was their private oasis, their slice of heaven.

He came around to help Savannah from the plane just as flurries began to fall.

"We'd better get a move on up the mountain." He grabbed their luggage from the back, then reached for Savannah's hand. She opened her mouth and closed her eyes, tipping her face up toward the sky. He watched her cheeks pink up from the cold as she caught snowflakes on her tongue. He could just imagine her teaching their child to do the same.

"You're going to be the perfect mom." He laughed as she turned a wide grin his way.

"Why? Because I'm such a child myself?"

He slung their bags over his shoulder and gathered her in close. "No. Because you never miss out on the little things."

"Put the bags down," she urged, tugging at them as they dropped to the ground. Then she held his hands and said, "Come on, Jack. Do it with me." She closed her eyes and tipped her head back again while he watched.

He had no idea how she knew he wasn't following suit, but without opening her eyes, she said, "Come on! Please?"

He opened his mouth and tipped his head back, letting the icy flakes melt against his tongue.

"Doesn't it feel good? I spend so much time in my law office that it's easy to forget what snowflakes taste like, or how it feels to dip our toes in a creek. That's why I do these things."

He opened his eyes and drank her in. She laughed as the flurries came faster, flaking on her eyelashes and wetting her cheeks. Jack took in the ground around them, now covered with a sparkling sheen of white, grass and dirt poking through here and there.

He kissed her chin, which was icy cold. "We should get up to the cabin and bring in firewood."

She sighed like a kid who wanted to stay outside and play. "Okay." She reached for a bag.

"Oh, no." He tossed the bags over his shoulders. "You've got more precious cargo to carry."

They made their way over the hill, and when the cabin came into view, Savannah stopped on the trail and leaned her hand on a tree.

"Savannah? What's wrong?" He was by her side, searching her eyes for signs of distress as she gazed out at the cabin with a smile on her face.

"I'm fine. Don't worry, Jack. You'll know if something's wrong. Look how beautiful it is up here tonight." She was breathing harder than normal, and Jack could tell she was trying to distract him from noticing it.

"It's gorgeous, but we need to get you inside." He reached for her hand and she clung to the tree, immovable.

"Just a sec. I'm really tired from the wedding." She was still smiling, but it didn't reach her eyes, making him worry. "Stop looking at me like that, Jack. I'm fine. It was a long day, and I'm allowed to be tired." She reached up and touched his cheek again. "Honey, I promise, I'm fine. Just tired." She pressed her lips to his and it took the edge off his worries. *Sort of.*

They headed inside the rustic cabin. The door opened to

the center of the living room–kitchen combination. A stone fireplace took up the wall to their right, and just beyond was a bedroom. They'd already planned to add another bedroom after the baby was born, but they had a while before they needed to expand their cozy hideaway, and they didn't want to worry about renovations while Savannah was pregnant. Besides, Jack and Savannah both wanted the baby to sleep in a bassinet in their room for the first few weeks, at least, so they could hear every sound he or she made. Jack dropped the bags by the front door and helped Savannah off with her coat and boots.

"Rest a bit." He helped her settle onto the couch. "I'll unpack."

He took the groceries they'd brought into the kitchen and put them away, then unpacked their bags in the bedroom. They kept clothing and essentials stocked for spur-of-the-moment weekends away, but he'd brought Savannah's favorite maternity sleeping shirt, her slippers, and other things he knew she'd want. Jack put fresh linens on the bed and tucked their empty bags in the back of the bedroom closet. When he closed the closet doors, he found Savannah standing in the doorway watching him. Her long auburn hair had grown thicker with the pregnancy and was draped over one shoulder. She looked sexy as hell fiddling with a lock of her hair, her big belly protruding under her maternity jeans and long-sleeved top.

"You're supposed to be resting," he said as he gathered her in his arms. "I was going to chop some firewood."

Savannah's eyes darkened and she licked her lips, sending heat to Jack's groin. She hooked her finger into the waist of his jeans and said, "I don't want to rest."

He tugged her in as close as her burgeoning belly would allow. "What did you have in mind?"

She worked the button free on his jeans and unzipped them. "Maybe we could play with *your* firewood."

He laughed under his breath. "You're so damn sexy." He wanted to seal his lips over hers and kiss her with all the passion burning inside him. He wanted to strip her bare, ease her sweet heat onto his rigid cock, and love her until she fell asleep in his arms, but he held back, worried about what he'd seen in her eyes a little while earlier on the trail. "I thought you were tired."

She slipped her hand inside his briefs and cupped his balls. "Never too tired for love." She palmed his eager length and stroked, slow and tight, driving him out of his fucking mind and stealing his last shred of control.

Their mouths came together fast and hungry. He rocked his hips against her hand to the rhythm of each stroke of their tongues. Her hand slid along his rigid length with practiced precision. She knew just how to take him apart. He drew her top over her head and rid her of her bra, setting her full, heavy breasts free. He filled his palms, brushing his thumbs over her taut nipples and earning a greedy moan from his voluptuous wife.

"You're so fucking beautiful," he said as he lowered his head to take one breast into his mouth. He licked and teased the way he knew she loved and was rewarded with another pleasure-filled moan as she tugged at his jeans.

Jack quickly undressed and carefully stripped Savannah bare. He kissed her intensely, cupping her face and angling her mouth so she opened further for him. They kissed the way night fell, slowly at first, then fast and all-consuming. He ran his hands along her ample hips, wider now than when they'd met. He loved the way her body accommodated the life they'd created. Savannah hadn't complained once about her pregnancy. She'd welcomed it, and they'd experienced all of it together, sharing in the joy of every pound gained, every kick of their baby. He kissed the swell of her full breasts and down the center of her belly as his hands slid along her thighs to the heat between her legs. He knew just how to take her up to the edge, and he took her in another deep kiss as he teased over her wetness.

"Jack," she whispered breathily. Her head tipped back and her nails dug into his biceps.

He nipped and sucked along her neck and felt her breathing grow shallow.

"Baby, you sure this is okay so close to the end?" He couldn't help it; he was nervous about anything that might set off early labor or cause her trouble.

"Jack!" She glared at him. "If you leave me hanging, I swear to God..."

He laughed.

She grabbed his wrist and held it exactly where it was. "The doctor said it's fine."

That was all the reassurance he needed to give her what she wanted. He stroked her sensitive nerves with his thumb as his fingers dipped inside, and seconds later she cried out his name, her inner muscles tightening around his fingers. She was so hot, so sexy when she came for him. He nearly lost it just watching her.

As the last of her orgasm shuddered through her, he led her to the bed and lay flat on his back, guiding her over him. They'd had to get creative these last few weeks, and holy hell did *creative* pay off. They'd made love standing, lying sideways, on chairs, bent over tables. Now, with Savannah straddling him, fully seated on his erection, he caressed her breasts as she rode him like never before. Her hair curtained her face, and she clung to his arms as she shattered around him again and again.

When she leaned back on one palm while cradling his sac with the other, her gorgeous belly reaching for the ceiling, he thrust in deep. Heat stroked down his spine, igniting the flames inside him, and he gave in to his own powerful release. Every thrust filled her with his love, until she came down over him, and he helped her lie on her side and held her close.

"I love those pregnancy hormones."

She laughed. "I think it's a Remington addiction. *God*, Jack, what you do to me. I love making love to you more than anything else in the world. I always have."

"I'm equally addicted to you."

He kissed her lips, then touched his forehead to hers, breathing in her essence, enjoying the blissful moment.

Chapter Three

WHEN SAVANNAH AWOKE the next morning, the fire Jack had started after dinner last night had already been tended to, burning warm and cozy in the fireplace, and Jack was outside chopping wood. She showered and dressed, then perched by the window watching him. Ogling him was more like it. She loved watching the muscles in his arms and back flex and bunch beneath his long-sleeved shirt as he swung that ax. It had snowed a lot last night, at least four or five inches, and she could see from the tracks in the snow that Jack had already gone to check on the plane. It was still coming down pretty hard.

She knew her husband well enough to realize that when he stopped cold every few swings and looked up at the sky, he was worried about getting stuck on the mountain. When they were dating, it had been fun to be stuck in the snow up here. They'd come just before snowstorms several times with the plan of getting snowed in. But that wouldn't do this close to the baby's birth. Jack would be a nervous wreck. In Savannah's mind, however, this was perfect. She still had at least two weeks, and probably more. What could be better than being here alone with Jack? She'd help him relax, like she had last night. God, she loved being close to that man. Everything he did, everything he said, made her feel loved and desirable. She'd never had a chance to worry about her changing body turning him off. From the very first few pounds she'd put on, Jack had lavished her body with love and attention, and she'd soaked it up.

He looked around again, then up at the sky, then back at the house. When his eyes found her, he feigned a smile. There was a big difference between Jack's forced smiles, which she knew were meant to put her at ease, and his real smiles—the ones that melted her heart. She couldn't wait to see Jack with their baby in his arms, safe and sound. She knew he'd always worry—about her, about the baby, about their safety. He was going to be an amazing father, and she knew all that worry would still be there, but it would just endear him to her even more. She understood why he worried so much. He'd lost so much already, and Savannah loved him enough to help settle those worries down. That was one reason she'd wanted to come to the cabin this last time before the baby was born. She wanted to love him up before the baby arrived and let him know how much she appreciated all that he did for her, for them.

The next time they came here, they'd have their baby with them and her attention would be divided between the two most important people in her life. The idea of sharing her emotions scared her. Did she have enough love to go around? Or would she always feel stretched too thin? She already loved this baby as much as she loved Jack, but the baby was still inside her and didn't require her full attention. She hoped and prayed she'd be as good of a mother as her mother was remembered to be, and as good of a parent as her father was. She had no idea how her father, as a single parent, had given each of his children so much attention while also running the ranch. She hoped parenting would be innate and that she was worrying for nothing, but she didn't want to let Jack down.

As usual, the thought saddened her. She'd been so young when she'd lost her mother that she only really knew her from descriptions and stories her father and brothers had shared with her. Even after her death, her mother's spirit had been kept alive through her father's and brothers' eyes. That alone told her what she'd missed out on by being born so near the time of her mother's passing.

Movement in her belly pulled her mind from those thoughts, and she smiled, pressing her hands to her belly.

Our baby.

Tears filled her eyes. These pregnancy hormones were going to do her in as badly as they had at the wedding. She needed to get out of the cabin or she was going to worry over what kind of mother she'd be all day.

She bundled up in her winter coat and tugged on her boots. She could barely bend over far enough to pull her boots on. At least the baby had sunk a little lower and was no longer living beneath her ribs. She could breathe easier, too. She just couldn't go very long without having to pee—which seemed like a good idea right now, too, before going outside.

After doing her business, she pulled her knit cap on, grabbed Jack's coat and gloves, and joined him outside.

He cocked a brow at her, stopping the ax midswing.

"Want to take a walk? I feel cooped up inside." She held out his jacket, and he set the ax down. A sweet smile lifted his lips as he piled wood in his arms, then leaned in for a kiss.

"Let me just put this inside. The snow's really coming down. We should stay close to the cabin."

She followed him inside and waited as he piled the wood beside the fireplace and secured the metal screen across the front.

"I think the mountain air will do me good. I'm a little edgy today."

He washed his hands, then wrapped his arms around her and kissed the tip of her nose. "Edgy? Like irritated edgy, or ready-to-have-the-baby edgy?"

"Like *I want to get out of the house and not think about whether I'm going to be a good mom or not* edgy."

He hugged her closer, and she breathed in his woodsy, masculine scent.

"You're missing your mom again, aren't you?" He gazed sweetly into her eyes as she nodded.

"A little." He knew her so well. Not for the first time, and definitely not for the last, Savannah was thankful she'd met a man who understood her emotions and who wasn't afraid to express his own.

"Oh, angel." His eyes warmed as he pressed his lips to hers in a tender kiss. "You're going to be the most amazing mother. You put everyone else ahead of yourself. Always. You love completely, with your whole heart. And you had the best role models a person could wish for. You'll see." He hugged her close, and her eyes dampened again.

Damn pregnancy hormones. "Thank you. I needed to hear that."

"Baby, your mom is smiling down on you, so proud of the woman you've become. I can feel it in my heart. You're probably just nervous because we're going to meet our baby soon." He rubbed her belly. "Baby Hallelujah." He smiled with the tease.

"You are *so* not naming this child."

A few minutes later they were bundled up and making their

way up the tree-lined trail hand in hand. Snowflakes continued to fall, giving the bright afternoon a crisp, magical feel. Long spiny branches wore rich layers of snow, like white gloves over graceful fingers.

"Watch your step," Jack said, when his heavy boot kicked a rock. He kept one hand on Savannah's back as they wound their way up the mountain.

When they reached their favorite overlook, Savannah felt out of breath. "Jack, I need to rest." Savannah stepped beneath the thick umbrella of trees that shaded the boulder where they usually sat.

"Hold on." Jack brushed off the snow and then eased her down. "We've gone far enough. I don't like you out here in the elements for too long anyway."

Savannah rolled her eyes. "I'm pregnant, not on my deathbed. You don't need to hover over me." She reached for his hand and pulled him closer. His broad shoulders split the sun, casting a shadow over her face. "I love you, and I love that you worry, but you've taught me to honor my body." She smiled up at him. "When I'm tired, I rest. When I'm hungry, I eat." She slipped her finger into the waist of his jeans, earning a seductive smile that softened all of her man's rugged edges. "And when I'm horny, I play with you."

He lowered his lips to hers and she tugged him closer, causing him to stumble. His hands landed on the rock on either side of her. He nudged her legs apart and moved between them. They fit so perfectly together, like two pieces of a puzzle. His tongue swept over the seam of her lips and she opened up to him, fisting her hands in his thick hair and deepening the kiss. She wanted to disappear into that kiss for the next two weeks, until they woke up with their baby in their arms.

Snowflakes cooled on their cheeks, and as their lips parted, snow fell harder. They both looked up toward the bright white sky. Jack's knit cap and the ends of his dark hair were covered in a sheen of white.

"We'd better head back." Jack reached for her hand, lifting her gently to her feet. Savannah's body swayed against him.

"Whoa." She settled her hands on the backs of her hips as a dull ache spread across her lower back. "I must have been sitting for too long. Hold on." She rubbed at the ache.

In the next breath Jack's strong hands were massaging the pain away. Concern was written in the grooves mapping his forehead. "Better?"

She turned in to his body, tightness remaining at the base of her spine. "Better, but it still hurts a little. Maybe I was sitting at a funny angle." She looked at the rock and smiled. "Remember the first time we made love? By the big rock that first night you followed me into the woods?"

His hands slid around her belly, and he nuzzled against her neck. "I'll never forget. That was the night you stole my heart."

He gazed into her eyes with so much love, her heart tripped in her chest.

"It sure didn't seem that way," Savannah teased, remembering how moody Jack had been the next day when he was teaching the survival class and they couldn't stop looking at each other. She'd known that all the emotions he felt scared him, and it had made her want to get to know him better, to ease his pain and to find out more about the rough and gruff man whose heart had been broken so badly he hid away from the world in order to survive.

"It was a difficult time. My heart was coming alive for the first time in two years." He pressed his lips to hers as they took a few steps out from under the protections of the trees and the density of the snowfall became evident. Snow fell in heavy sheets.

"Shit. Come on, angel. I need to get you home." With one arm secured around Savannah's waist and a firm grip on her arm, he led her as they descended the mountain.

Their footprints on the trail were already gone. Jack knew the mountain like the back of his hand, expertly maneuvering around trees and rocks, even without the trail to follow. The tension in Savannah's back eased and returned in progressive waves. She slowed her pace each time it returned.

Remembering a conversation she'd had with Max about this sensation, she said, "I think these are Braxton-Hicks contractions."

Jack stopped cold, his eyes filled with worry as they dropped to her belly.

"Contractions? But you have two weeks, at least."

"Braxton-Hicks," she repeated. "Remember I told you what Max said? They're like practice contractions. She had them for three weeks before giving birth to Adriana." She pressed her hands to her belly and smiled up at Jack. "My body's just getting ready."

His eyebrows knitted together. "You sure you're okay?" He looked out at the snow. "I don't think it's safe to fly in this, but if you need a doctor—"

"Jack, I'm fine." Knowing what she was experiencing made the waves of dull aches easier to handle. "Come on. Let's go back to the cabin. Maybe I just pushed too hard today."

The trek back down the mountain usually felt much faster than the walk up, but today, with the snow and the new bodily sensations, Savannah moved slower. By the time they reached the cabin, it was late afternoon, they were both sweaty—Savannah from carrying all the extra baby weight and Jack, she was sure, from pure concern—and Jack was in full doting mode, hovering over every move she made.

He helped her out of her coat and boots, taking each piece of wet clothing off carefully in front of the fireplace so she stayed warm. Her maternity pants and sweatshirt had remained dry beneath her jacket and boots. He settled her onto the couch and removed his own soaked clothing and boots.

"Where do you want to rest? The couch or the recliner?" he asked as he disappeared into the bedroom, returning with her favorite thick blanket, fluffy slippers, and her e-reader.

Her heart squeezed at his thoughtfulness as he knelt to ease her feet into her slippers.

"This is fine," she said, settling back against the cushions.

Jack spread the blanket over her and moved the footstool closer. He placed her feet gently on the stool.

"Water?" he asked, already on the move to the kitchen.

"Jack, relax. I'm okay, really."

He set a tall glass of ice water on the end table and sat down beside her.

"What else do you need? Want me to rub your back? Your feet?"

"Jack." She loved the nurturing side of him, but he was making her nervous. "I just want you to sit with me and chill out."

"I can't help it. I know you said these are practice contractions, but what if they're real?" He looked out the window as the sun set. Snow was coming down so hard, it was difficult to see past it.

"Then I wouldn't be able to sit here so calmly. Remember

what Max said? She said real contractions were like being kicked in the back by a horse." She felt her smile falter. "Ohmygod, Jack. Please remember to tell the doctor that I want an epidural if I'm too far gone with pain to ask for it."

He drew those broad shoulders back, confidence replacing the worry in his eyes, as he brushed her hair from her face. In the space of a second, her *rock* had returned.

"Don't worry, baby. I'll be right there with ice chips, asking for an epidural." He smiled and pressed his lips to hers. His voice softened as he spread his big hand across her belly, then lowered his face and said, "I can't wait to meet you, Baby No Name."

She laughed. "Let's think about names. What do you think of Sophia for a girl?"

"I like it, but what about Adeline? It's close to Adriana for your mom, and we could call her Addie." He rubbed her belly, and his hand stilled. "Aren't there any names you dreamed of calling your children when you were little?"

"I didn't dream of babies and white picket fences—you know that. I dreamed of horses and…You know what? I don't think I spent a lot of time dreaming. I was too busy keeping up with my brothers to worry about the future. Of course, once I was a teenager, I was dreaming about becoming a lawyer, but this?" She placed her hand over his. "This dream only became real when I met you.

"What about you?" she asked, immediately regretting the question. She didn't want to dredge up sad memories for Jack, but they'd always been open and honest about the loss of his wife and that they had been planning for a baby.

"I want this baby to represent *us*, all that we love, all that we've given to each other. I'd name a little girl Savannah if you'd agree, but you've already nixed that one."

She smiled. "I know you would. I don't need a baby with my own name." She cuddled in against him and closed her eyes, realizing that the waves of tightness in her back had finally eased. "I think I need to nap."

"Do you want something to eat first?"

She shook her head. "No. You go ahead. I'm too tired."

SAVANNAH SLEPT FOR several hours. Jack ate dinner, brought in enough wood for the next few days, and tried to call his parents, but with the storm, there was no cell reception. Snow was now coming down at a blinding rate. He hoped that by morning it would let up. He'd already decided that as soon as it did, they were flying back home. He wasn't going to take a chance of getting stuck on the mountain in another flash storm. When Savannah had said the word *contractions*, all he could think was that he'd failed her. They were at the cabin in the middle of a snowstorm, and her doctors were forever and a day away, back in New York City, where they lived. He knew she needed this time away for just the two of them. The cabin had always felt a world away from their real lives back in the city, where Savannah's legal practice awaited. He wondered how many times her best friend and coworker, Aida, had tried to call over the past twenty-four hours. She and Aida were thick as thieves, and he knew Aida was on pins and needles about the baby, just as they were.

He tossed another log on the fire and stretched out on the recliner, keeping a close eye on Savannah, asleep on the couch. Truthfully, he'd wanted this time away just as badly as she did, but now it was time to go home. Time to get his wife back to civilization, where contractions wouldn't cause him heart palpitations, because her doctors were just a phone call and a short cab ride away.

Savannah was sleeping soundly on her side, with a pillow tucked between her knees. Her hair was spread across the cushions, and Jack swore he'd never seen anyone smile in their sleep as much as Savannah did. He loved that about her. She was such a positive light in his life, and had been since the day they'd met. Oh, she was stubborn as a mule. He thought she got that from her father, Hal, but Hal swore she was exactly like her mother had been. Savannah was also tender and loving, and she was always pushing Jack past his comfort zone, making him a better man, which was another thing he loved about her.

Jack dozed off, listening to the crackling of the fire and the even cadence of Savannah's breathing.

He startled awake in the middle of the night, unsure of what had woken him. The cabin was dark, the fire burnt to embers. He tended to the fire, adding more wood to keep them warm, and heard Savannah moan in her sleep. He set the screen before the fireplace and knelt beside his sleeping wife. He didn't want to wake her. She'd been so tired after their walk; she really needed to rest. Once the baby was born, they'd be up every few hours at night, and though he knew she'd enjoy every moment with their new baby, he also knew she needed to get as much rest as possible before the birth.

She moaned again, a long, drawn-out, painful sound that brought his hand to her waist, hoping his touch would settle her back into sleep and out of whatever was causing her distress. He felt her belly tighten, and his breath caught in his throat.

Practice contractions, he assured himself. *That must be what's causing her moans.* Waking her would do no good. Instead, he rubbed her gently, hoping to ease the tension.

"They've been going on for a while," she whispered in a strained voice.

"What can I do?" Jack caressed her cheek. "Do you want to move to the bed to be more comfortable?" He pulled his cell phone from his pocket. Still no service.

Savannah sat up, breathing deeply. "I'm okay. Sorry I woke you."

"Baby, don't ever worry about me." He pressed his lips to hers. "Just tell me how I can help. Did Max give you any ideas about what to do when you have these?"

She shook her head. "She just said to breathe through them and know they'd pass. As I was lying here, I remembered that the doctor mentioned that, too." She glanced at the window. It was pitch-dark outside. "Is it still snowing?"

"It was when I fell asleep. Come on. Let's get you out of your clothes and into something more comfortable. Maybe that'll help you fall back to sleep." He helped her from the couch, and she clutched his arm with both hands, sucking in air between her teeth.

"Wait."

Jack's heart raced as he held her up. "Babe?" He watched her sweatshirt move with the contraction. "Are you sure these are Braxton-Hicks?"

She huffed a few loud breaths before answering. "How should I know? This is my first baby."

"Okay, angel. Let's try to relax and—"

"Relax? How can I relax when my belly is getting tight and hard like that?" she snapped, eyes wide with fear or annoyance—he couldn't tell which.

"Baby, I just meant that we should get you in the bedroom and make you more comfortable, that's all. I didn't mean it like, *chill out*." He knew how much his wife hated being told to relax in *that* way.

"I'm sorry," she said as he wrapped an arm securely around her waist, guiding her toward the bedroom.

"Let me help you get your pants off." He smiled as he said it, biting back the urge to tease her about sex and try to lighten the mood. She was too edgy for that. She leaned on his shoulders as he knelt to remove her pants. He tossed them onto the rocking chair in the corner of the room and went to the dresser. "What do you want to sleep in?"

"My big T-shirt."

"Okay." He grabbed her favorite maternity sleeping shirt and helped her take off her sweatshirt. She stood before him in her panties and bra, looking more beautiful than any lingerie model ever could. She was carrying their baby, the child their love had created. What could be more stunning than that? His throat thickened with emotions as he unhooked her bra, freeing her full breasts.

"Christ, Savannah. Even eight and half months pregnant, every part of you turns me on." He placed her hand on his erection, and she trapped her lower lip between her teeth.

"Jack," she said softly. "Oh, shit." She squeezed his crotch—hard.

"Fuck." He moved her hand to his arm and held her as the contraction tightened her belly, the sharp pain in his balls she'd caused forgotten.

"Breathe, Savannah. It's okay, baby. Breathe." She was huffing and puffing so fast he feared she'd pass out. His brain kicked into gear, drawing on what they'd learned in the childbirth classes they'd taken.

"Look at me, baby. Focus on my eyes." She did. "Good. Breathe with me. In…" He drew in a breath. "And out." He blew it out slowly, repeating the steps until the contraction passed and her breathing calmed.

"Good girl." He slipped the T-shirt over her head and helped her put her arms through.

"Jack?"

He heard the fear in her voice before he caught it in her eyes. "It's okay, baby. I'm right here. These are practice contractions, remember?" At least he hoped they were.

"I know, but…" Her eyes dampened.

He folded her into his arms and brushed a soothing hand down her back. "I'm here, angel. I'm right here, and there's nothing we can't handle. You're okay. I promise." He drew back and searched her eyes. "Talk to me, baby. What are you afraid of?"

She opened her mouth to speak and no words came, but tears slid down her beautiful cheeks, slicing his heart wide open. He gathered her in close again, pressing a kiss to her cheek.

"You're going to be an amazing mother, and we are going to be such a happy family." He helped her lie on the bed and stripped from his jeans, then slid beneath the covers behind her and held her close. "I've got you, baby, and I'll never let go."

Her hand clutched his arms as another contraction swallowed her up.

"Jack," she cried.

He tried to move away to rub her back, but she gripped him even tighter.

"Stay. Hold me."

"I'm here. I was just going to massage your back."

She shook her head. "I need you close."

Damn right he'd stay close. He didn't quite believe these were *practice* contractions.

Chapter Four

SAVANNAH DOZED IN and out between contractions, and Jack, true to his word, held her the entire time. He'd encouraged her to let him rub her back, but she was too scared to move out from his embrace, despite the worsening pain. She needed to feel his strength enveloping her, his breath on her neck, his heart beating strong and sure against her back. She didn't know what time it was when that dull ache in her lower back circled around to the front and engulfed her with so much force she cried out, but the room was still steeped in darkness.

Jack jumped to his feet, scanning the room. "What? What happened?"

She gritted her teeth against the pain of the contraction as he came down beside her and lifted her gently, bringing her back against his chest. He rubbed soothing circles over the sides of her belly, but the pain was too much. She couldn't stand his touch—any touch. Even the bed beneath her was annoying her.

"Stop!" She pushed away. "Ohmygodohmygodohmygod. Jack. These can't be practice contractions."

Jack flicked on the light, his face serious. She knew that face. It was his *taking stock of what they needed* face. "You're sure?"

Another contraction slammed her back against the head-board. "Shitshitshit. Jack."

He climbed onto the bed beside her. "Look at me, Savannah. Remember, we need to breathe."

"We?" She breathed fast—too fast, trying to stay ahead of the pain.

"Yes, *we*. Focus on me." His words were stern, though his eyes were full of love. He breathed in a calm pattern until she matched his breathing. "You're okay. Together we can do whatever needs to be done."

Her contraction eased, and as if he'd been waiting for that moment, he jumped off the bed, reached for his jeans, and dug out his phone. "Still no service."

"What do we—ohmygod!" She doubled over with another contraction, and Jack drew her back up again.

"Breathe. Good girl. In and out. Good, Savannah. Good girl." He held her trembling hands as she breathed through the contractions. When the contraction subsided, she felt like a train had run through her and left her ragged.

"I need to get a few things before this gets any more intense, okay?"

"What? Where?" Her brain wasn't working right. She was anticipating the next contraction and afraid of him leaving.

"I need to boil water so we have it sterilized and get a few towels. It's okay, honey. I'll be back in two seconds." He kissed her quickly, then raced out of the bedroom.

She listened to the water running, the pot filling, the sound of the stove lighting. The refrigerator opened, then closed. She heard him talking fast, and seconds later Jack was back at her side with a stack of fresh towels and a bowl of ice.

"I can break up the ice with a hammer." He rubbed her

back.

"Jack, is this it? Do you think this is it? I'm not ready. Anything can go wrong. We need to go back to New York." She moved to the edge of the bed to get dressed, and he gripped her arms and held her steady.

"There's a foot of snow outside, and it's still coming down. We're not going anywhere. I put a call in with the emergency radio, but it'll take forever for the team to get here."

"A foot...Oh God. Jack. We're stuck in a snowstorm and I'm going to have our baby and we have no doctor and—"

He wrapped her in his arms and lifted her chin, holding it in place as he stared back at her with love and confidence in his steady gaze. "And we will be fine. If this is it, if our baby wants to arrive today, tonight, whenever, we'll bring him or her into the world safely. I will not let anything happen to either of you."

She watched him swallowing hard and knew this must be even harder on him, having already lost one wife at the time when they were planning their own family. She wanted to tell him that if anything bad happened, it wasn't his fault, but that brought up the idea of something bad happening, and that was too hard to even think about, much less say out loud. She saw a hint of fear wash over his face, and just as quickly it was gone and her rock had once again returned.

"I KNOW YOU won't, Jack."

Savannah's voice drew him back to the present from the momentary slip into darkness. He pushed away all thought except for what was happening right here, right now.

"Do you want to walk or rest?" he asked.

"I don't know. I don't want to overreact to—" She squeezed his arm as another contraction hit.

"Breathe," he reminded her—and himself. As he breathed with her and the contraction eased, another one hit, and another was right on its heels. The magnitude of the situation hit him full force, and he was on his feet, settling her on the bed as he drew back the covers. "I need to get the water so it can cool."

He quickly brought the water into the bedroom and set it on a chair close to the end of the bed, mentally ticking off what else they'd need. He hammered the ice and offered Savannah ice chips, then soothed her through a few more contractions. His mind reeled a hundred miles an hour, as he pulled from every pregnancy and childbirth reference he'd ever read, of which, over the last eight months, there had been many. He could do this. He'd had enough medical training to keep her safe, and for the love of his life, and their unborn child, there was no way in hell he was going to fail.

"We need to get your underwear off to see if this is progressive labor," he said hurriedly.

She wiggled out of her panties and put her feet flat on the bed, letting her knees fall open. "God, this feels so weird."

In an effort to ease her worries, he said, "As long as I'm down here," and wiggled his eyebrows.

"Jack!" She laughed. "What do you see? Is the baby coming?"

He tried to focus, but it took him a minute to understand what he was actually looking at. The area around her vagina was bulging. He could see a wide swatch of the baby's head. The pit of his stomach clenched tight. This was really happening. Their baby was coming. He remembered reading about asking the mother not to push hard until the baby crowns.

"I need to wash my hands again. Whatever you do, don't push." He tore out of the room with Savannah's voice trailing behind him.

"Jack? The baby's coming!"

He scrubbed fast, all around his nails, in between his fingers, everywhere he could as quickly as he was able, and ran back into the room. Savannah's face was scrunched up tight, her eyes slammed shut.

"Breathe, Savannah. Please, breathe through this. Tuck your chin. Good girl. Now push, but not too hard. You don't want to tear." He widened her knees and remembered reading about massaging the perineum. How the fuck did doctors do this? His hands were shaking badly as he silently prayed for his wife and baby.

"The baby's coming. Jesus, Savannah. I couldn't love you more than I do right now. You're so brave." Her private parts were spread wider than he'd imagined possible. The word *miracle* swirled in his mind.

"Jack!" Another contraction engulfed her.

"Okay, you need to push, baby. Grab beneath your knees and hold your legs back." He hoped he was doing this right, but how many ways could there be to deliver a baby? It had to come out.

Savannah groaned. "Hurts! I can't!"

"You can, Savannah," he said sternly. "You can and you will. Breathe. Good girl. When it's too intense, exhale through your mouth. I remember reading that you should push hardest when the contraction eases."

"I can't. I have to push!"

The baby's head was crowning. With his heart in his throat and every ounce of him hoping he was guiding her in the right way, he said, "Okay, push."

Savannah groaned and grunted, her face deep red.

"Breathe, angel. You have to breathe, too."

"Shut. Up." She pushed again, and the baby's head turned as it came through, facing downward.

Jack's heart nearly stopped.

"Stop pushing! Stop! Stop! The umbilical cord is wrapped round the baby's neck." He worked quickly to unwrap the cord, being careful not to pull on it, while Savannah shouted his name over and over, crying, begging for details.

"Okay. It's okay. You're okay." He couldn't find the right words; he was too focused on getting the baby safely out. "It's good. The baby's good."

Another contraction hit. "Jack!" she yelled as she bore down.

"It's coming, angel. You're doing it. Savannah, you're doing it. You're incredible." Tears streamed down Jack's cheeks as one of the baby's shoulders popped out, then the other, and then the baby slid into his waiting hands. "It's…Savannah, we have a baby boy. Oh my God. He's perfect."

Jack and Savannah both cried as he grabbed a towel with one hand while cradling their baby with the other, then dunked the towel into the sterile water, quickly cleaning the fluid and mucus from the baby's mouth and nose. The first cry was like a sound from the heavens above, and as the baby screamed, he noticed the cord and followed it back to her body. Hell, she still needed to deliver the afterbirth. He placed the baby on her belly, safely nestled in Savannah's capable hands, as he helped her. With the baby still attached to the afterbirth, because in his frenzied state he'd forgotten to sterilize scissors, he laid their baby in her arms and went to work cleaning up his amazing wife and their incredible little boy.

He quickly removed the bloody towels and blankets, replacing them with clean, dry ones, and then, with both his wife and their child clean and warm, he joined them at the head of the bed. He kissed Savannah's tears from her cheeks, kissed her lips, her forehead, her hands, all the while telling her how much he loved her. The love he felt for her and the baby was bursting from him in every way it could. He lowered his lips to the baby's forehead. They counted each of his fingers and toes, and Jack swaddled him in a clean blanket, feeling their bond sink into his heart and become part of his soul.

"He has your hair," Savannah whispered. "Jack, we did this. We made this beautiful baby boy."

Emotion clogged his throat. He opened his mouth to speak, but his words were swallowed by the love inside him. He wiped his tears, watching Savannah as their son latched onto her breast for the first time, and he felt complete in a way he'd never imagined he would.

"Angel," he finally managed. "You amaze me." He kissed her again. "Look at him. Look at you."

"Jack, you did this. You brought him into the world with me. You unwound the cord from his neck. You saved our baby's life." She smiled up at him with fresh tears in her eyes.

Those words, and the love in her eyes, bowled him over. For fear of falling apart completely, he tried to joke his voice from his lungs.

"See? He should be named baby Hallelujah."

She rolled her eyes. "What do you think of Adam James Remington?"

"Adam James." He liked the way the name rolled off his tongue. He looked down at their perfect little boy suckling his mama and whispered, "Adam James Remington." He smiled. It felt right. "I think I love it."

"I know he's going to be big and strong like you, and he's our firstborn, so Adam fits." She leaned down and kissed Adam's forehead.

"You want to honor my father?"

She nodded. "It feels right to. He's a good man, Jack."

"What about your father?" Jack asked. "We should honor him, too."

"We did. We gave him the most gorgeous grandson on the planet."

"Thank you," he said, unable to quell the emotions tugging at him. "Thank you for bringing me back to my family when we met and for loving me enough to stick by me when I was so broken."

"You were never broken, Jack. You were mourning. There's a difference." She leaned in for a kiss, and he met her halfway.

Adam's tiny pink lips unlatched from Savannah's breast, and together they placed their tiny bundle of love upright on her chest to help him burp. When that little sound came, fresh tears sprang from their eyes.

Jack wiped her tears and pressed his lips to hers, knowing that all he ever needed was right there in that room.

—Want More Bradens & Remingtons?—

Read more about Jack and Savannah in BURSTING WITH LOVE (The Bradens).

Sign up for Melissa's newsletter to be notified of new releases, giveaways, and special events.
www.melissafoster.com/Newsletter

New to the Love in Bloom series? Love in Bloom is a big family romance collection featuring several families. Characters from each series appear in future Love in Bloom books. All Love in Bloom books may be enjoyed as stand-alone novels or as part of the series.

~ Love in Bloom Series Order ~

Snow Sisters – Book 1 FREE
The Bradens – Book 1 FREE
The Remingtons – Book 1 FREE
Seaside Summers – Book 1 FREE
The Ryders | Harborside Nights
Wild Boys After Dark | Bad Boys After Dark

Find family trees, reading order, and more on Melissa's Reader Goodies page.
www.melissafoster.com/Reader-Goodies

Get the essential Love in Bloom Series Guide to keep track of your favorite characters, and take notes on engagements, marriages, and births.
www.melissafoster.com/LIBSG2

More Books By Melissa

LOVE IN BLOOM SERIES

SNOW SISTERS
Sisters in Love
Sisters in Bloom
Sisters in White

THE BRADENS at Weston
Lovers at Heart
Destined for Love
Friendship on Fire
Sea of Love
Bursting with Love
Hearts at Play

THE BRADENS at Trusty
Taken by Love
Fated for Love
Romancing My Love
Flirting with Love
Dreaming of Love
Crashing into Love

THE BRADENS at Peaceful Harbor
Healed by Love
Surrender My Love
River of Love
Crushing on Love
Whisper of Love
Thrill of Love

43

THE BRADEN NOVELLAS

Promise My Love
Our New Love
Daring Her Love
Story of Love

THE REMINGTONS

Game of Love
Stroke of Love
Flames of Love
Slope of Love
Read, Write, Love
Touched by Love

SEASIDE SUMMERS

Seaside Dreams
Seaside Hearts
Seaside Sunsets
Seaside Secrets
Seaside Nights
Seaside Embrace
Seaside Lovers
Seaside Whispers

BAYSIDE SUMMERS

Bayside Desires
Bayside Passions

<u>THE RYDERS</u>

Seized by Love
Claimed by Love
Chased by Love
Rescued by Love

SEXY STANDALONE ROMANCE

Tru Blue
Truly, Madly, Whiskey

BILLIONAIRES AFTER DARK SERIES

WILD BOYS AFTER DARK
Logan
Heath
Jackson
Cooper

BAD BOYS AFTER DARK
Mick
Dylan
Carson
Brett

HARBORSIDE NIGHTS SERIES
Includes characters from the Love in Bloom series
Catching Cassidy
Discovering Delilah
Tempting Tristan

More Books by Melissa
Chasing Amanda (mystery/suspense)
Come Back to Me (mystery/suspense)
Have No Shame (historical fiction/romance)
Love, Lies & Mystery (3-book bundle)
Megan's Way (literary fiction)
Traces of Kara (psychological thriller)
Where Petals Fall (suspense)

Meet Melissa

www.MelissaFoster.com
www.MelissaFoster.com/Newsletter
www.MelissaFoster.com/Reader-Goodies

Having sold more than a million books, Melissa Foster is a *New York Times* and *USA Today* bestselling and award-winning author. Her books have been recommended by *USA Today's* book blog, *Hagerstown* magazine, *The Patriot*, and several other print venues. Melissa has painted and donated several murals to the Hospital for Sick Children in Washington, DC.

Visit Melissa on her website or chat with her on social media. Melissa enjoys discussing her books with book clubs and reader groups and welcomes an invitation to your event.

Melissa's books are available through most online retailers in paperback and digital formats.

Made in the USA
Middletown, DE
14 September 2018